THE VANISHING

A SHORT STORY IN
THE DYING LANDS CHRONICLE

JACOB COOPER

The Vanishing

AUTHOR'S NOTE

In many instances as I write the next installment of the Dying Lands Chronicle, new threads of the world's history arise and demand to be explored. Such was the case with *The Red Grove* (now part of the expanded release of *Circle of Reign*), and *Remnants and Shadows* (now part of the expanded release of *Altar of Influence*). *The Vanishing,* first published in the *Journeys* anthology put out by Woodbridge Press, is no different in its genesis. It started coming to life as I was writing *Song of Night,* book 2 in the Dying Lands Chronicle (and yes, that installment is coming). Here, the story has been a bit reimagined and expanded. I hope you find it a thrilling origin story that gives greater depth to the people of Våleira and their history.

Finally, if you have not read the expanded, rewritten versions of *Circle of Reign* and *Altar of Influence*, I *highly* encourage you to do so prior to the release of *Song of Night.* But for now, I hope you lose yourself completely in *The Vanishing.* Let me know what you find.

~*Jacob Cooper*

THE VANISHING

ONE

1,007 Years After The Fracturing

DELANIS, THE FOURTH THRONE OF ISHALAR, knelt on the gray sand, tracing a shallow human footprint, a child's, before the surf could wash it away. He imagined warmth still rising from the impression despite the wind whipping off the chilled water like icy knives, tearing through his blue woolen tunic and thick kilt as if they were paper.

They had vanished again, The Sick, tracks ending at the edge of the sea, as always. This time they had left at night.

His hand crumbled the edge of the footprint as he closed his fist, trying to stifle the anguished bile rising in his throat. These traces would fade. The charred shadows The Sick left behind in the village would not. Small crabs nibbled at his knuckle with their pincers before the next swell of surf chased them into their shallow places of refuge. To the northeast, the seven Isles of Skithya lay splayed across the angry surface of the sea like petrified remains of the Immortal Ones. A lonely gull cried overhead as it sailed upon the currents of the wet morning air.

"There are more here," Kirth warned in a throaty voice, almost a growl. Delanis's brother stood roughly twenty paces away, presumably referring to another set of footprints. "Deeper than the rest, with a hard cut on the outside. Probably Baelor's. Poor fat bastard. His prints are staggered, like he was drunk."

Delanis did not move, still staring at the small, delicate print before him. It held him, and he knew why.

Orra.

His daughter, now well into the clutches of The Vanishing, felt The Luring hourly. Something called to The Sick, pulled them. And Delanis knew his daughter's time drew nigh—he could feel it. She grew more restless every day, every hour. Delanis had held Orra—limp and trembling—all night, daring whatever took The Sick to come and tear her from his strong arms. But he knew something hadn't *taken* The Sick. *The Luring,* he thought, that unfathomable force that pulled The Sick into their watery graves. Even now, Orra remained tied to the bed in her chambers. That hadn't stopped others from vanishing, but what else could he do?

Delanis ignored the cold water of the next wave as it erased the footprint he had traced, bubbly foam skimming around his knees. The undertow stole the sand beneath his knees and even that small, seemingly insignificant loss of support brought on a brief sense of falling. He reached a hand forward to catch himself, marring the dark sand that the retreating wave had just smoothed.

He closed his eyes. The cries of gulls filled his ears and the briny aroma of the sea rose in his nose. Normally, those familiar elements would have cradled a peace deep within him, but today they did not assuage his desperation. How long would it be until he would find Orra's small footprints in the sand?

Delia, goddess of nurture, hear my plea….

A heavy hand on Delanis's shoulder roused him.

"Come," Kirth urged. "We must report to the First Throne."

"Gaerrin can wait." Delanis exhaled ponderously as he stood. "How many?"

Kirth pursed his lips. "Seven sets of tracks, I think."

Seven more from their lands had disappeared. Seven more lost to The Vanishing.

Delanis scanned left and right, noting the other sets of tracks. "They are spread wide . . . far from each other."

Kirth nodded. "They always are."

"But why enter the water alone?" Delanis asked in frustration. "Are they not aware of each other?"

Kirth shook his head, jostling the trinkets of bone woven in his beard. "I'm not sure why this matters."

Delanis turned away, staring down at a piece of driftwood. "I'm not sure that it does. I just. . . I just need to understand, brother. Why do they leave? Why not stay and die in their homes? Why drown themselves?"

"I do not know these things. But I will stand guard on the beach every night for Orra. I swear it by the Five Thrones. If you watch her in your home and I keep the vigil here, we're sure to stop her and the others."

"You were on the beach all last night, Brother. You and four others." Delanis's words did not have the bite of accusation in them, simply fact, and he turned to catch Kirth's eyes. "I do not blame you, but I can't lose Orra as well. I can't. Not after her mother . . . I just can't." Delanis heard the desperation in his own voice. His wife, Selirra, had succumbed to The Vanishing just four cycles past, in the middle of the high season.

"I know, Delanis," Kirth said.

"This isn't some enemy we can attack," Delanis groused, his frustration rising. He grabbed the hilt of the short blade at his waist. "Not something we can kill with steel or arrow. No griptha can cure this. Believe me, I've thought about entering the holy pact of vengeance to seek Vyath's guidance . . . but the gründaalinas sent me away from his altar. 'How can the god of war help you fight an invisible enemy?' they ask, ignoring the fact that he lives in the realms of the invisible." Delanis raised his eyes to the sky. "And Delia . . . she refuses to hear my pleas for nurturing and healing."

"I see the helplessness pooling in your eyes, brother. Cast it out. You must be strong. Do not doubt the gods."

Delanis again studied the other sets of tracks. They spanned nearly the entire beach. His eyes narrowed in thought. In the distance, Farfin, the shipbuilder, hammered planks into submissions along the hull of his latest creation. The dampened thuds of his mallet against the wood barely made it to Delanis's ears above the wash of the surf. Something caught in Delanis's mind.

"The tracks . . . Kirth, the tracks converge."

Kirth raised his eyebrows. "No, they don't. They span the entire beach."

"They would converge if not for the waters. Look!"

Delanis pointed and then ran to the set of tracks nearest him. With the heel of his sealskin boot, he carved a line to the water's edge, along the angle of the tracks. He repeated this with the next set of tracks. After several minutes, all seven sets had lines drawn in the sand, tracing their trajectories.

"What are you doing, Brother?" Kirth asked, his head cocked, eyes blazing into Delanis as if peering through a disguise.

"We need twelve others," Delanis said. "Round them up, along with seven long lines of rope, at least a hundred paces each, and a long stake."

"Delanis, you're acting mad."

"Just do it, Kirth! And bring that Hardacheon who's visiting Throne Gaerrin."

"Girshkil? That mad babbler who's always counting stars at night?"

Delanis nodded, staring into the ocean. "Yes. Him."

TWO

WITHIN AN HOUR, TWELVE VOLUNTEERS gathered on the beach around Delanis, seven men and five women. The men wore fur cloaks, woolen kilts or pants, and fur-lined sealskin boots. Thick beards hid most of their faces, and some had trinkets of bone woven into them—trophies from conquests and raiding. The women, faces as grim and downtrodden as the men's, wore long, woolen dresses with fur shawls wrapped around their arms and shoulders. Girshkil, the Hardacheon mad babbler, stood a bit removed from the group, mumbling something inaudible as he tapped a finger in the air. Kirth dropped seven coils of rope at

Delanis's feet, the scowl on his face glistening with a sheen of sweat.

"There are fourteen of us, not including the Hardacheon," Delanis said. "And seven sets of tracks. I've carved a line next to each set that shows the general direction of the footprints. I want one of you standing at the head of each line of footprints, holding one end of a rope, and the other seven to follow those lines into the water, holding the other end of the rope. For those walking into the water, the one at the head of the track line will keep your trajectory true."

"To what end, brother?" Kirth asked.

Delanis saw the same question on the faces of the other volunteers. Wind nipped at the hems of the women's clothes as it tore from the sea. "I'm not sure. It might be nothing. Just trust me for a few more moments."

Girshkil's head snapped up, his eyes calculating. "Interesting." His air-tapping finger picked up speed.

"What is?" Kirth stammered. "Vyath's blood, I already have chills between my shoulder blades. Delanis, you better start explaining why I'm going into the freezing water for you, or by the Five Thrones, I swear—"

"He thinks they converge and create a new trajectory," Girshkil said. "You don't see it?"

The confusion knitting Kirth's thick eyebrows turned to astonishment. "I thought you were mad, Brother, when you said you wanted to take up farming over raiding. Are you seriously saying you think The Sick *went* somewhere? Through the sea? They killed themselves, Delanis! The madness took them, and they ended it."

"But why the water?" Delanis asked. "Why not a blade? Why not leap from the Ovis Cliffs? Or hang themselves from the trees of the black orchard? And why, in all Eyrna's mercy, do we not ever find their bodies washed up along the shore?"

Kirth shook his head. "Madness."

Still, the brawny man did as his brother requested and, along with five others, waded into the water with Delanis, each of the seven tracing a separate line of tracks into the sea as they held onto the end of their individual ropes. The water seeped into Delanis's boots slowly at first, but the surf soon washed over the top edges. He shivered as an aching numbness settled in his calves as he pressed on. Turning back toward the beach, he looked at the woman, Phidla, standing at the head of his set of tracks. She motioned with a stiff arm for him to move right. He did so. On the beach, Girshikil measured the distance between the set of tracks.

He does see what I'm seeing, Delanis thought.

Delanis had taken roughly seventy steps when he ran into one of his volunteers. Their tracks had intersected.

"Stop," Delanis said. "Are you in line with your set of prints?"

The man peered back to the beach, squinting at his counterpart. "Yes, my Throne."

Delanis checked his line. Phidla signaled that his trajectory was true. He saw Kirth and the other volunteers making their way forward, on a direct intercept course toward his position. The water reached just below Delanis's shoulders.

One by one, the other five converged on the exact same position. "Each of you, pull your lines taut," Delanis ordered. "Kirth, the stake."

Kirth pulled out the stake, thick as his arm and nearly as tall as he stood.

"Drive it deep, here," Delanis said, pointing. "Right where our paths converge."

Kirth did so, twisting and pushing the sharpened point of the stake into the seafloor. Then, he pounded the stake deeper with the flat back edge of his ax.

Girshkil rushed into the water, his lips moving, presumably mumbling his incessant babble. He had two fingers tapping the air now, trying to push his way through the shore break.

"How did the Immortal Ones ever let him survive the womb?" Kirth asked. The gods were supposed to take the lame and the daft from the womb, give them a merciful stillbirth. "Their Influence must have waned more significantly since the Fracture than we thought."

"The Nine Clans fractured over ten centuries ago," Delanis explained as Girshkil drew nearer, awkwardly splashing. Delanis shivered. "I don't think the Immortal Ones exist anymore."

Girshkil pushed past the group and pointed southeast, a nervous whine on his tongue. "There!"

Delanis followed the Hardacheon's gesture. He squinted to make anything out along the gray-water horizon.

"What, there?" Kirth grunted through clenched teeth.

Delanis felt the irritation bubbling within himself as well as he shivered against the chilled water. Farfin had wandered over to the group on the beach, no doubt the odd sight of seven fools pulling rope into the ocean drawing him from his labors.

"That is where they would have gone," Girshkil said. "Assuming a plane with no friction or loss of mass upon intersection, the confluence of the seven vertices would create a new trajectory in roughly *that* direction." Again, he pointed, triumphantly, a bit to the southeast. "It's about impulse and conservation of momentum. Clan Makenshale, one of the Nine Immortals, taught this before the Fracture. See, when the intersection occurs—"

Kirth grunted. "Can I kill him yet?"

Despite his chattering teeth, Delanis managed a smile. "Maybe later," he said, "but for now, we need to go see Throne Gaerrin."

FOUR

DELANIS, KIRTH, AND GIRSHKIL stalked through the main thoroughfare of Heina, the seat of the Five Thrones and the largest settlement in Ishalar. Homes of stone and stout wooden roofs covered in reeds bordered the cobblestoned thoroughfare on either side, growing sparser as the hills west of Heina rose into view.

Wrapped around Delanis's shoulders, a thick woolen blanket shielded him from the wind's bite at his wet clothes. He shivered despite the blanket. A light snow had begun to fall, and small eddies of crystalline precipitation danced in front of them.

Farfin, the shipbuilder, joined them on their way to speak with Gaerrin in the Hall of Thrones.

How much longer will we remain free? Delanis wondered. As if The Vanishing were not challenging enough, the Borathein pressed upon them from the west. Between Ishalar and Borath stood Ashid, Kjïln, and Valcar. Rumors fluttered in the air that Fatheim of Hevlik, north of Borath, had bent the knee to the Borathein deklars last rising season. Diplomatic relations were the concern of the Second Throne, war that of the Third Throne. Still, though outside his stewardship as Fourth Throne, the rumors could not help but trouble Delanis.

Along the streets of Heina, families smoked the morning's catch—a haul of horned salmon. The scent made Delanis's stomach groan. He hadn't eaten in a day at least, sick with worry for his daughter. Around the corner of the next street, he knew what he would find: a charred shadow on the outer wall of Baelor's house. Berry juice darkened the outside walls of seal paste and lichens, but the shadow still stood out prominently.

Delanis tried to look away as he passed Baelor's home but failed. Baelor's grieving family and others gathered around the sooty aura and burned small bundles of fewla in remembrance, taking in the bitter aroma. Flowers and small offerings mounded at the foot of Baelor's shadow as the women spoke soft words of hollow comfort to his wife. His son, Goshan, only thirteen, appeared well on his way to achieving his father's girth. The lad bravely held back his pooling tears.

Ishalite men did not cry.

But Delanis had cried when Selirra succumbed to The Luring; and again, last night, silently, as he hissed accusing prayers to Delia with Orra, weak and lethargic, in his arms.

Something else gnawed at the edge of Delanis' worry as he came upon the scene outside Baelor's home. He smelled ash, something burning other than fewla. A white crust outlined Baelor's charred shadow and the tincture of something like burning glass tainted the air. In Goshan's hand, a wooden bucket with a burlap handle swayed slightly, a thick rivulet of white paste dripping slowly down the side.

Plaster?

"Throne Delanis!" Baelor's wife, Mishya, called out through a sob.

Delanis stopped and closed his eyes. He knew what would come. *Vyath take me, I cannot help.*

"What happened?" Delanis asked, motioning to Goshan.

Mishya glanced toward her son briefly. "He tried to whitewash the shadow away. Crushed oyster shells and whale oil. But . . . " Mishya's lip trembled.

"It burned through, didn't it?" Delanis asked.

Mishya nodded. The shadows, or whatever they were, did not allow themselves to be hidden. Delanis, after fruitlessly scrubbing for hours, had tried to cover Selirra's shadow on the floor of his home for Orra's sake—or was it his?—with a bear skin, but the floor covering had smoldered to ash wherever it touched the shadow's outline within moments. That acrid scent of burning fur still rooted itself in Delanis's mind.

"Throne Delanis," Mishya whispered. "Why won't the gods hear our prayers? I gave offerings at Eyrna's and Delia's pantheon faithfully." Her hands shook as she spoke. "Why? Please, tell me! The grüdaalinas say we have angered Vyath and the other gods cannot tame his wrath. What must we do?"

Delanis turned to face her. "Mishya, I am sorry for your family's loss. I know the pain all too well."

"People say," she said, sniffling and wiping her chapped nostrils, "you found something on the beach. Is this true?"

Delanis sighed inwardly. "No. Just the footprints again, like always. I am sorry."

Mishya closed her eyes and let the tears fall. Goshan stomped into their small home and slammed the door so hard that one of the hinges broke. Along with the sound of the boy's yelling came the clamor of things breaking.

"Could you invoke a blessing upon us?" Mishya asked. "Please. Just one of comfort?"

"The Fourth Throne is quite pressed," Kirth said. "He must not be delayed further."

Delanis could not imagine anything he might say that would bring comfort. His Immortal Eye now slumbered, had refused to awaken for some years, the same as with the other Thrones. But, for pity's sake, he could at least lie for Mishya's benefit. What could a few false kind words hurt?

He touched his hand to the woman's forehead and she closed her eyes, a whisper-thin thread of relief seeming to rest upon her. Upon finding the link at the bridge of her nose, Delanis dared to hope that his Immortal Eye would—no. No Sighting opened to him. He sighed inwardly.

"Mishya, by virtue of the authority of the Thones

of Ishalar, I invoke a blessing of comfort and peace from the Immortal Nine upon your home. Know that your good husband suffers no more and rejoices in the Immortal Halls. He waits for you. Can you see him there?"

Mishya's jaw quivered as she exhaled.

"Can you see him there?" Delanis repeated, gently.

"Yes," she whispered, her eyes still closed.

"Your faithfulness will see you to his side once more when the Immortal Ones call you home."

Mishya reached up and touched Delanis's wrist and forearm. "Thank you." A thin stream of a tear escaped her closed eyes.

He and his company left the grieving family and continued toward the Hall of Thrones.

"Did you see him when you invoked the blessing?" Kirth asked. "You know, Baelor? In the Immortal Halls?"

"No."

"What did you see?"

"Nothing, Kirth. Just the darkness." He gazed down the road toward the Hall of Thrones, sighed, and then spun on his heel. "I'm going to see my daughter. Throne Gaerrin can wait. We need to change out of our frost-ridden clothes anyway." As if to accent the point, he pulled on the front of the fur cloak that wrapped around his shoulders and covered the top of his chest, and it came away from his body with a crisp crack, like bark being torn from a tree. "Farfin, your new ship, when will it be ready?"

The shipbuilder, bald but for a stubborn tuft of hair the color of wet sand, grunted a reply. "Half a day if I have help."

Delanis nodded. "You have my leave to press as many into service as you need. And keep it quiet. I want to leave at midday, Farfin, not a moment later."

Farfin nodded and hurried off.

"What are you about, Brother?" Kirth asked.

"Meet me at my home in an hour."

FIVE

WIND CAUGHT THE SINGLE SAIL on Farfin's ship, the lines thrumming under the tension, the timbers of the ship groaning. After getting underway just past midday, Delanis had ordered the crew to row out much farther than normally required before hoisting sail, an attempt to remain undetected for as long as possible. Their absence would be noticed before long, if it had not been already. He knew Gaerrin would come for them.

"How is she?" Kirth asked, stepping to Delanis's side near the stern.

Orra lay on the deck wrapped in thick blankets, her head on Kertsin's lap. Kerstin gently hummed a longing lullaby.

Five Thrones, where is the sun? The whirlpool-shaped clouds of the season hid even what cheer the sunlight might have brought to Delanis. Nightfall would soon cast her shroud upon them.

"Unchanged, Brother," Delanis said. "Worse, perhaps."

"Eyrna will have mercy. You will see."

"Your faith in Eyrna instead of Vyath is ironic," Delanis said.

"I kill quickly. Little suffering. Is that not merciful? Is that not of Eyrna?"

Delanis's smirk turned to a smile and he chuckled. "What I wouldn't give to see the world through your eyes for a season."

They sailed south by southeast, toward the glacial lands that harbored nothing but desolation.

"What does your Sight tell you we will find?" Kirth asked.

"I cannot say."

"You must have some idea. You have seen things."

"I am not sure I trust my Immortal Eye, Kirth." Delanis pursed his lips and spoke softly. "It has slumbered for so long. I do not dare trust it fully. What if . . ." He paused. "What if whatever causes The Vanishing has interfered with the Sight of the Thrones? What if we are heading into a trap?"

Kirth appeared troubled. "You doubt the blessings of the Immortal Ones? Is Sight not of them? Now whose faith is ironic?"

"I had you bring twenty of our strongest, did I not?"

"If you think a threat awaits us, why not have brought this to Throne Gaerrin?" Kirth hissed. "We could have come with more force."

"Brother, I am not certain what awaits us," Delanis said. "But I know Gaerrin would not have let us go. And you might be right. This whole journey might prove a waste. Perhaps The Vanished truly are simply dead."

"But why?" Kirth asked. "Why would Gaerrin not support you if it meant hope of an answer?"

"Because the needs of Ishalar are his first priority, as mine are supposed to be. He would see my leaving as a distraction at best and treachery at worst. And he would probably be right."

"But you are a Throne. Would he not—"

"Kirth, Gaerrin and I are not friends. He would not have listened. I have put my personal needs above that of Ishalar and pressed you and others to follow me. I am selfish in this. Forgive me."

"Politics and I would have never mixed," Kirth said roughly. "I have only the mind for the ax and shield. I'm glad you were born first."

"Don't be ridiculous. You would have consolidated all Five Thrones under you within a week through assassination."

"Vyath's blood, I would have. If we survive this, I still might."

Two warriors, their beards heavy with bone trinkets, turned their gazes toward Delanis and Kirth. Delanis shifted his weight.

"Perhaps a different conversation would—"

Orra started moaning, rocking slightly in her sleep.

"Shhh, sweet girl," Kertsin whispered. "You're safe, you're safe . . ."

The moans turned to wails. Delanis rushed to his daughter.

"She's cursed!" one of the men, Heyak, cried. He pointed accusingly. "She has to be thrown overboard!"

In a move so swift that Delanis barely saw it, Kirth pounced on Hayek, slit the man's throat, and threw him overboard. Kirth's motion flowed seamlessly, one fluid graceful movement that belied his size.

"No!" Delanis yelled too late as Heyak hit the water.

"Anyone else want to suggest giving my niece to the sea?" Kirth asked, Heyak's blood dripping from his short blade down his kilt. "Eyrna's mercy, I just had this kilt made!" He wiped futilely at the wet stain.

"Kirth," Delanis said, his tone serious, "this—"

"I know, my Throne. I apologize . . . to a point. He always irritated me something fierce."

Delanis shook his head with his mouth open. "Then why did you bring him? His bragging about our journey nearly allowed Gaerrin to intervene and—"

"I . . . well, I hoped an opportunity might . . . you know. Present itself."

Orra sat up, as if pulled by an invisible rope anchored in the center of her chest. Her head lagged behind the motion, finally catching up to her torso and swaying lazily atop her neck, as if she were drowsy. Blankets sluffed off her, revealing her simple white shift that clung to her sallow skin, soaked through with sweat. Her eyes locked straight ahead on some point out of sight.

"She knows you're coming." Orra spoke slowly, her words raspy and weak.

Delanis knelt in front of his daughter, but her eyes refused to find him. She continued to stare at whatever commanded her attention, something beyond the horizon.

"Orra," he said. "Orra, what is this you speak? Who knows we're coming?"

Her head continued to bob with an unnatural slowness. "Mother."

Black birds—ravens?—had gathered on the yard across the top of the sail like rats flocking to bloated corpses. He searched the sky to see where they had come from, and saw more winging toward them, but could not see whence they came, almost as if the thin air birthed them. The unkindness of ravens flocking to the yard buzzed or hummed—Delanis could not tell which—with a discordant refrain. Despite the taut sail brimming with wind, the ship's momentum stalled.

Farfin ran to the starboard side of the ship and peered down. "Fractured Nine, there's no wake." He raised his hand above his head. "Or wind."

Delanis rose, wary eyes locked on the unkindness, the yard bowing at the ends slightly as more ravens coalesced, streaming from some unknown origin. In a frenzied display of nervous vying, the ebony legion turned violent. They clawed and pecked, screeched and shrieked; long black feathers, thick with blood, spiraled to the deck.

The ship's timbers protested loudly as the breezeless wind—or some eidolonic presence—pressed more severely into the sail. A rope snapped. The stay line whistled sharply, ending in a crack as it tore across a sailor's face. Amid the man's cry, a pinkish pulp oozed from his eye socket. Another line snapped, the sound akin to a frozen lake cracking underfoot.

Everyone dropped to the deck, covering their heads. Delanis shielded Orra and Kertsin with his body.

A *howling* rose from what sounded like the belly of the ship.

"Delanis!" Kirth's voice. "Do you feel it? The deck!"

Delanis turned his head, still covering Kerstin and Orra. From the corner of his eye, he saw Farfin prone with his ear flat against the deck, not cowering from the peril of scourging lines but concentrating. Listening.

"What is it, Farfin?" Delanis whispered. The howling increased, rising in pitch and volume.

"The ship . . . it feels angry."

"Angry? The ship?"

Ravens, bloodied and broken, pelted the deck now as the fray atop the yard reached a climax. More fell, the dull thuds of their impacts adding an incongruous rhythm to the atonal howling. That smell of wet rust found Delanis's nostrils as frantic men scrambled for whatever cover they could find, smearing avian ichor under their hurried feet. A raven landed on Delanis. Foam bubbled from the bird's beak, its head hanging limply at an unnatural angle. Delanis slapped it away.

"Yes," Farfin said. "The wood vibrates. Almost like the ship itself is—"

"Howling." Delanis hadn't heard it, his head not close enough to the deck as he shielded his daughter, but he guessed Farfin's meaning.

Against the forward gunwale, Girshkil whimpered as his finger tapped the air incessantly. He hugged his knees against his chest as the man seemed to try to make himself as small as possible. He jerked as a raven thudded beside him, the bird twitching in nervous spasms, pushing itself in circles with a broken wing, before falling still.

The world around Delanis seemed to smear suddenly, losing its focus. He blinked, then rubbed an eye to no effect. Black striations streaked away from the dead ravens, red striations from the blood, brown from the masts, white and tan from the sails, and a translucent gray from the water itself, like stiff steam. All the striations flowed in the same direction, like frayed silk teased by a congruous wind.

Delanis held a hand up and saw the striations pulling away from it, as if something tore at his skin. Even the white shift his daughter wore fuzzed, ghostly thin white threads streaming away from it, as if it were being unsewn.

"What . . . what is this?"

"I hate this part," Girshkil muttered. "I hate this part, I hate this part . . ."

A new sound entered the cacophony, and Farfin's head snapped toward the mast. "No . . ."

Delanis pivoted, following Farfin's gaze. The mast craned toward the bow at a dangerous angle with the sail still drawn taut from the spectral wind. Sanguineous splatters stained the sail in streaks of scarlet. Just as Delanis felt certain the mast would snap, the sail tore, relieving the pressure.

The mast straightened.

The howling faded to nothing, like the death of a whispery echo.

The ravens dispersed, fleeing in every direction, save for the dead.

The striations disappeared.

And the wind, the natural gales of the world, returned.

Upon wobbly knees, Delanis climbed to his feet. He didn't have the words to break the blessed yet eerie silence. No one did, it seemed. Kirth proved him wrong.

"Farfin, have you named this new ship of yours yet?"

Visibly shaken, the shipbuilder just shook his head.

"Well," Kirth said, "I think the Red Raven feels most apt."

"Delanis?" Kerstin called.

He turned to her. The same question in her eyes swam within him.

"I don't know," he said. "I just . . ."

Through a light haze, a white mountain emerged from the mist ahead. Slowly, it came more into focus, and Delanis saw that it was not a mountain, but a floating glacier with a crevasse so large that it masqueraded as a covered fjord. First moon rose from the southern horizon, its bluish light skimming the sea's surface.

"How?" Farfin asked. "We weren't moving."

"Even if we had been, we should still be a full day out," Delanis said. "We can't be there yet."

"The world folded around us, of course," Girshkil said. "Did you not feel it? Oblivion? How I do hate it when that happens."

"I have no idea what you're talking about, Hardacheon," Delanis said. "Speak plainly." Then, thinking better of it, he said, "Never mind. Just, don't speak at all."

"How do you think the Ancients moved across the world so quickly? You found a rift. They are so few now since The Turning Away."

"The what?" Kirth asked.

"He means the Fracturing," Delanis answered.

Kirth faced the babbling madman. "You should have let me kill him on the beach, Brother."

"Orra!" Kerstin shrieked.

Delanis spun to Kerstin. With a hand covering her mouth, she pointed toward the bow. Where Orra had sat, an ashen sediment stained the deck planks dark. Dread seemed to hang from his head like a pendulum, forcing his gaze to sway in the direction

Kertsin pointed against his will. Atop the bow figurehead, Orra stood, her loose shift flapping in the wind.

Without turning, she spoke, her voice sounding as if a dozen doppelgängers whispered all around them. "I told you, Dada. She knows you're coming. They all do."

Orra plunged into the sea.

"No!" Delanis cried. "Kirth, a line!"

Farfin and Kirth grabbed a rope and threw one end to Delanis. He tied it around his waist.

"Why isn't she surfacing?" Kerstin asked. "Orra!"

"Hold the line, Kirth," Delanis ordered. He climbed upon the rail.

"The Fractured Nine can have that!" Kirth said, stepping up to the rail beside his brother. The large man jumped in before Delanis could object, no line attached to him.

"Go!" Farfin yelled, holding the other end of the rope.

Turning back to the icy water, Delanis saw ripples marking his brother's entry point. None marked Orra's.

He jumped. The chill shocked him as he hit the surface, momentarily freezing his muscles and wiping his mind of all coherent thought. His lungs clenched. He forced the broken pieces of his focus to reassemble. *Orra.*

Down he dove, struggling to get full range of motion from his contracted muscles. The dim light of evening disappeared into cold nothingness. Still, he dove deeper, ignoring the acute pressure building in his ears. He reached into the nothingness, farther and deeper, waving his arms more desperately. He prayed his hands would graze any part of Orra. Her shoulder. Her flowing hair. Her innocent face that beamed with Eyrna's grace. But no, his flailing hands found nothing, and his lungs burned with furious need. He would not relent, so deeper he swam, demanding his lungs withhold their need, that his ears resist the pressure, that his cramping muscles obey his will and—his lungs released their air and involuntarily sucked in.

Dark water flooded them. In pure reflex, Delanis coughed out the water and then drew in a bigger breath, his lungs ballooning with the cold blackness. Suddenly, the cold of the water seemed to depart, as if it had been an illusion, to be replaced by a comforting warmth.

He felt his consciousness slip, detaching from reality like cobwebs releasing their tenuous hold against old trusses. And then, he slid fully into the void.

Delanis woke and found himself standing upon frozen ground, wispy tendrils of wind-blown snow snaking around him, slithering just above the ice. Around him he only saw more of the same desolation, it seeming to appear from nothing as his vision reached the utmost bounds of its limits. His eyes stung, like when he used his Immortal Eye to grant him Sight. The air shattered as something shrieked above him, some roar with the tenor of an avalanche rushing down the mountains of Valcar mixed with the ominous pitch of a white eagle. Delanis felt a warning. He dropped face-first to the icy ground and felt the air change above him, the sound of something like loose sails amid mighty gales.

Wings.

A shadow streaked across the ground so fast he only saw a fading glimpse. The creature did indeed have flight, if he saw it right, boasting a wingspan larger than any white eagle. Delanis scrambled to his feet and ran for any cover, any outcropping to shield himself. The avalanche-roar sounded again and a feeling of falling spun in his stomach. He dove, stretching himself long as he slid. His face burned as the frozen earth bit his bare skin. The burning spread down his shoulders and chest.

I'm naked, he realized. It was then that he finally felt the cold while his chest and face burned from the rough ice. Again, he felt the air change above with the sounds of large wings. He closed his eyes.

Delanis did not feel the piercing of talons or the gauging of a beak, as he expected. Tense moments passed. That mineral aroma of cold filled his nose with his shuddered breaths. When he dared open his eyes, he craned his neck to look forward. Feet clad with talons, a thick body covered with matted bluish-gray hexagonal scales, and a maw with bony protrusions at the chin filled his vision. Oval eyes, dark like pits of coal but burning with a wild fury, glared back at him. Its densely feathered wings drew close to its body as it loomed as tall as a warhorse and then half again. Delanis stepped back. The creature made no advance.

What are you?

Warily, the creature turned its back to Delanis, its head peering over its shoulder. The beast's neck must have been twice as long and thick as Delanis's arm, the same length as its tail that sprouted a round boney mass at its end.

"What do you want?" The question left Delanis feeling daft, speaking to an animal. *A demon from the Plains of Kulbrar, no doubt.*

Alysaar.

The word came unbidden to his mind. And, not in the flavor of his thoughts. It *tasted* different, like the morning. But that wasn't quite right, was it? No . . . incomplete. It tasted of the vaporous dew upon budding leaves in a clear morning of the rising season mixed with the simultaneous promise of quintessential and quiescent currents from the apex of the world upon which to glide and the feverish heartbeat of prey squirming with reflexive but hopeless desperation. Exquisitely delicious.

Things moved toward Delanis, black shapes seemingly just below the surface of the frozen ground. They . . . they had the bodily form of people. Limbs shot out from an inky center mass and extended toward him. Animated shadows. *Living* shadows. The ground steamed where the shadows flowed beneath it, the ice turning gray then black, rocks turning to brittle ash. A profane scent rife with the acrid tincture of burning flesh assaulted his nose. Delanis recoiled, his chest going tight. Clawing and reaching, the shadows moved in freakish, disjointed actions, seeming to pull themselves through the cold, translucent earth, almost as if they were swimming.

Mount.

Again, the thought entered his mind unbidden. He turned toward beast—the *alysaar*—and it lowered its hind legs.

Mount.

Did he dare? The shadows drew closer. An innate fear prickled over him, and his vision shook. Yes, he dared to mount the beast. Delanis dashed toward the alysaar, but the ground vanished. Gone. His foot pierced the now-nothingness below him followed by his body. He tumbled, flailing as he fell into whatever new terror he had stumbled. Violet lightning split the alabaster sky and the wind whooshed in deafening gusts as he plunged further still into the void. Below him, folds of gray and brown with patches of dark green materialized into land, mountains. They rushed up to meet him. Delanis screamed.

Something streaked past him from above, a scaly lithe form swooping beneath him. Wings unfurled, arresting the creature's dive as they caught the air. When he hit the alysaar's back, Delanis blacked out.

Seek me, Throne Delanis of Ishalar. I will make your blood sing with new life.

He tried to look, turning his head this way and that, but could see only blackness.

That voice, like . . . like a song. A melody. More pure than anything he had ever experienced. It also had a taste, though, at the edge of his sensitivity. Bitterness.

Why can't I see anything? he asked the voice.

Because your eyes have not yet been opened, Throne Delanis of Ishalar. Seek me and be granted true Sight. Seek me, seek me . . .

SIX

THE CREAKING OF BRINY-SCENTED WOOD. The soft groan of lines drawn taut, bristling against their anchor points. A gentle rocking, the languid swaying of the ship. The sound of surf sloshing against the keel. Even the cry of a gull far off, though it sounded thinner than normal.

Delanis, supine on his back, opened his eyes to splotches of light. The illumination was not overly bright but still stung his eyes. Against his will, his eyelids fell shut. With renewed determination, he opened his eyes again. By and by, the picture focused. An unseen light source glowed a dim blue luminescence above him, seemingly all around him, as if he had entered an azure cocoon. His eyes fluttered, trying to determine what he actually beheld.

"He's awake."

A soft voice, one he knew. When he spoke, his words tasted of salt, his throat rough like sand. "Kerstin . . ."

"Shh, my Throne. Do not strain yourself."

Delanis swallowed and grimaced from the briny taste. "Orra."

"Shh," Kerstin whispered.

"Where . . ."

"I could not find her, Brother," Kirth said, kneeling beside him. "I found you on my way up. I was almost out of air. Tugged on the rope. The crew hauled us out of water. Orra is . . . with her mother now."

"Perhaps," Delanis said.

"You heard her. She said Selirra knows you're coming, then jumped into the water."

"She called her Mother."

"Aye," said Kirth, slowly, like a parent to a child.

Kerstin's stiffened and Delanis saw realization come over her. "Orra always called her Mama. Never Mother."

"Not once," Delanis said.

"What are you saying?" Kirth asked.

"I heard a voice. I think it was female . . . but not human. It was too . . . perfect."

"Was it part of a Sighting?" Kerstin asked. "Let me see your eyes."

Delanis stared at her. She nodded. "The white lightning still abides in your irises."

He turned away. "This is more than we know. This is no sickness, this vanishing. Something is harvesting our people."

The blue cocoon had sharpened in his vision, and he thought he saw a crack at the top, through which small pricks of light twinkled.

"Where . . . are we?" he asked.

"In the crevasse," Kirth said. "The babbler insisted it was the right way."

Yes, Delanis saw it now. The blue was that of glacial walls unspoiled by sunlight, the indirect light that of first moon. He curled himself up off the deck, attempting to rise. Kertsin protested but Kirth helped him to his feet. Men sat at the oar stations, their strokes slow and hesitant, propelling the ship at near wakeless speeds. The sail had been struck, Farfin and another man working on mending the tear.

"What is that?" Delanis asked, wiping his eyes. "There, in the walls."

Kirth pivoted. "What?"

Could he have imagined it? "It looked like . . . a star." His voice bounced back at him, coming too fast to be an echo. The crevasse bestowed an uncanny stillness in the air.

"Perhaps the light from first moon?" Kerstin asked. "Shimmering off the walls?"

There, something twinkled and raced up a crease in the ice wall beneath its surface, just ahead of them off the port bow. It disappeared nearly as fast as Delanis had seen it. The color was wrong to be a reflection of first moon. More amber, like the golden fields of grain he dreamed of growing for his people.

"No," Kirth grunted, his tone wary. "I saw it. Or, I think I did."

Girshkil rose from his spot against the gunwale. Another flash streaked up the wall to the starboard side. "There is no time," he mumbled. "No time, no time."

"I have seen these before," Delanis said. "In a Sighting."

"What?" Kirth asked. "When?"

The others on the ship appeared startled, taking note of the phenomenon. More flashes streaked up the walls, mostly yellow, some a bright green, dragging a hue of deep blue at their tails.

"When my Eye opened with Orra. I was given Sight of these . . . Lucents."

That word had also come to his mind unbidden, a similar taste to those of the alysaar.

"What do they mean?" Kirth asked. "Are they hostile toward us?" He took the ax from his belt. Immediately, the blue tails turned to a dark crimson. Their frequency increased.

"I'm not sure," Delanis said. "But perhaps we should lower the ax . . . at least until we understand more."

"Why is it always that you want to now turn away weapons instead of use them?" Kirth sighed and put the ax back in his belt. "I liked the old Delanis."

Even in the face of losing Orra to The Luring he still can be lighthearted. Delanis did not fault his brother for this, but rather harbored a healthy envy. The ship hugged the crevasse wall to the port side. "Bring us closer," he said.

The port oarsmen drew in their oars and the ship crept closer to bluish-white ice.

"Easy," Farfin whispered, more to himself, as if guiding the ship's momentum. "Easy, now."

Delanis reached his hand out and grazed the glacier's surface. Beneath his touch, the ice streaked with yellow and green Lucents. No warmth or other sensation came to him, just the flickering beauty of the strange yet mesmerizing currents that danced all around him and the crew within this glacial cocoon.

"It is like something trapped the northern lights of the night sky in the fourth low cycle," Delanis said. His hand traced the wall as the ship glided forward, feeling its alternating rough and smooth textures, its flat and jagged sections. He looked up and saw the night sky through a crack in the fjord's ceiling some hundreds of feet above. The opening could not have been more than two boat widths.

And then he remembered. *The shadow!*

Delanis stomped to where Orra had been, where he had seen the beginning of her shadow forming. It was not there. He rubbed his fingers along the deck planks and took away the barest film of soot. He breathed relief as he worked the soot between his fingers.

"What is it?" Kerstin asked.

"Orra is still alive."

"How do you know?"

"Her shadow did not fully form."

Kerstin placed a hand on his shoulder and spoke gently. "We don't know—"

"I do," Delanis snapped, then softened. "I'm sorry." He took her chin in his hand and kissed her forehead. "I know she's alive. This is a good thing, her shadow not appearing fully. I'm not sure why, but I feel it. Please trust me."

The light of the Lucents danced across Kerstin's face. "I do," she whispered.

The Red Raven—Farfin had indeed chosen that name—drew near the exit of the crevasse. Girshkil huddled in his spot in the forward gunwale, his fingers twitching. "I hate this part, I hate this part …"

The rift . . . we never left it. This is some kind of reprieve.

The Red Raven neared the exit of the crevasse. Howling again rose from what seemed like the hull of the ship. A current snared them, sucking them into a swelling tide that rose without warning.

"This is different," Farfin said, grabbing one of the gunwales.

Delanis felt the stern rise. He turned to see a wave surging, its crest opening like a foaming maw.

"Row!" Farfin barked.

The oarsmen dug their wooden blades into the water with feverish abandon. The howling increased.

"We're not going to outrun this," Delanis yelled. The spray of the angry wave flecked his face as he stared it down. "Brace!"

The Red Raven pitched forward as the wave slammed into its stern. The jolt clattered Delanis's teeth, and he grabbed the stay rigging with one hand, Kerstin with the other. Two men launched into the air, their screams muted by the violent swells as they hit the water. Delanis did not see them resurface as the ship surged forward. Wind whisked his hair and beard straight back, tugging on his scalp and face. Oars snapped and shot free from their holds. Debris impaled Farfin's leg, jutting out the other side like a stave. He slid down the deck as the ship reached a precipitous downward angle and slammed into the forward gunwale next to Girshkil.

Delanis pulled Kerstin closer into him. He shielded her as best he could from the maelstrom and held firm on the steering arm. Beneath him, the ship bucked as the wave hurled it recklessly toward the narrow exit. It grew larger in Delanis's vision and the howling now drowned out even the surging torrents. Kerstin shook in his arms, muttering something. A prayer. He tasted the tang of fear in the back of throat. Breath would not come, but he could not look away.

It seemed that all strength left Delanis's legs as the wave spewed the ship through the crevasse's exit so narrow that he thought he could reach out and touch the frozen edges as they shot through. With the stay rigging hooked into the crook of his arm, he sunk to the deck, still holding Kertsin.

The suddenness of the silence felt like pressure, like Delanis was again underwater. When he dared open his eyes, unnatural becalmed waters greeted him, like blackened glass stained by first moon's bluish-white gleam. Just above the water's surface drifted a lazy haze.

A noise, somewhere ahead of them, cut the silence. It had started so faintly that Delanis hadn't realized he was hearing anything for several moments. He stood, raising Kerstin to her feet.

Clank. Clank. Clank.

Almost a whisper, the staccato, unflinching rhythm pulsed in the air. Farfin hobbled to his feet with Girshkil's help near the bow. They bound Farfin's wound as best as they could.

Clank. Clank. Clank.

All aboard the Red Raven stared toward the sound's provenance, a point in the mist that seemed to swirl in place.

"It's coming closer," Kirth whispered.

Delanis hadn't sensed his brother's approach. "What is it?"

Kirth took the ax from his belt. "Iron against wood."

The mist parted off the port bow, cut by the keel of another vessel about a hundred boat lengths from them. Delanis squinted. On that vessel, dozens of people beat the flats of axes and swords on rails, the butts of spears on the deck, all in unison to the tempo of a calm heartbeat. Delanis's pulse raced. The people . . . they were not people anymore. Their sallow skin, the bulging purple veins beneath their eyes—these were The Vanished, reappearing like ghosts from the Plains of Kulbrar. And then the clanking's volume climaxed, impossibly loud for those on the new vessel to cause alone.

Delanis looked up. *My Sighting . . .*

The fog thinned, and Delanis saw hundreds of people, thousands even, dotting ledges that spiraled up the sides of glaciers not ten boat lengths from them.

The Vanishing was no sickness. Delanis knew that now. It was a *calling,* a clarion tolling that drew from all across the world. They had sailed into the den of The Vanished.

"How many are we?" Delanis asked.

Kirth briefly scanned their ship. "Eleven, if I don't count the Hardacheon idiot."

"Farfin," Delanis said, taking his own ax and short blade from his belt, "can you fight?"

"Run, no," Farfin said. "Fight, yes."

Delanis turned partway to Kerstin. "I'm sorry I let you come."

She took two shields from over the railing and passed one to Delanis, then drew a medium-length sword from her provisions. "It was not your choice. I would do it again."

The ship of The Vanished lumbered nearer. Every clank shook Delanis's joints, rattled his bones. Above the ship, ravens circled.

I told you to seek me, Throne Delanis of Ishalar.

He went rigid. That voice again . . . so melodious. Was he the only one to hear it?

Submit, and live.

His eyes stung fiercely, his Immortal Eye glaring into the void. *Who are you?* he silently called. *Show yourself!*

Only the worthy may see me, Throne Delanis of Ishalar.

Who are you? His mind shouted the words.

You may call me Mother, She who Fractured the Immortal Clans, She who freed Entropy from the Living Light's prison, She who will see the Resurgence come to pass and sow Entropy back into the elements of the world.

Delanis reached deeply into his Sighting, his eyes burning as if lightning truly scorched his pupils. *Your name, eidolon!*

Noxmyra il'Helosha, Mother of the Ancient Darkness. And you, Throne Delanis, are my kin.

"Noxmyra . . . il'Helosha," Delanis mumbled to himself.

"How do you know that name?" Girshkil snapped. "How do you know *that name?*"

Clank. Clank.

"A Sighting. She says I am her kin."

Girshkil seemed to weigh something in the precious seconds that fled as the ship of The Vanished closed in. "Yes," he said finally. "The Ishalites have the blood of Clan Helosha, the clan that brought about The Turning Away, the Fracturing of the Nine Clans in your history. Chaimere il'Kiarra, the last of the Ancients, of your Immortal Ones, has sent me to your people, to watch. For, it is believed among some of us that your bloodline is more susceptible to the Ancient Dark. It would appear that this theory is true."

"And The Vanished?" Delanis asked.

"Those whose blood has been changed, who are now sustained by the Ancient Dark instead of the Living Light, Entropy instead of the Lumenatis."

Delanis's mind spun. "I do not know these words you speak. But it seems we must kill this Mother."

"No," Girshkil said. "She is not in the world but seeks Her return to it. The veil holds her."

"The Resurgence," Delanis mumbled.

Girshkil's eyes widened in surprise. "She speaks to you?"

Beware him, Throne Delanis of Ishalar.

Delanis nodded.

"Then," Girshkil said, eyes darkening, "I am sorry." He drew a blade from his robe and hurled it at Delanis with such speed he barely had time to duck beneath his shield.

"Vrathia!" Girhskil cried.

The blade struck the shield, and it exploded, leaving only the leather grip and a couple of dangling pieces of broken wood.

Vyath's blood, what is this?

Kirth sprinted toward the Hardacheon, ax

raised. Girshkil didn't even try to dodge. "You must not live, Throne Delanis, for the world's sake. Your gift is of the Light, but your blood is tainted by the Ancient Dark. You will become a conduit for the Dark."

Before Delanis could even think, Kirth lunged forward, ax swinging, and nearly took Girshkil's head off in one swipe. The Hardaceheon slumped to the deck with a thud.

Delanis stood, heart thudding, in shock. A grappling hook hit the deck of the Red Raven with a clang, then the line attached it snapped taut. Others followed. Savage cries rose from the ship of The Vanished and echoed off the glacial walls. Kirth and the remaining warriors slashed the lines but more grappling hooks bit into the railing, pulling the ship toward The Vanished.

"Let it come!" Kirth said. He beat his ax against his chest.

The vessels collided. The first Vanished leaped to the Red Raven and met the back edge of Kirth's ax. The Vanished's skull caved under the blow, and the man fell overboard. Two more Vanished leaped across, swinging axes wildly. Delanis finally got his head into the battle, ducked and countered, lodging his ax deep into a chest. Still the attacker came, undaunted. More Vanished crawled over the Red Raven's rails like famished rats, their motions rabid and rigid.

Delanis kicked the dead Vanished, freeing his ax. Kerstin battered a Vanished with her shield, forcing it back. Her lunge saw her sword into the its gut, but the creature still came at her, impaling itself further. Delanis buried his ax in its head, and it finally succumbed.

Kirth swore. Delanis turned to see his brother pull a spear from his own shoulder and turn it on his attacker. Two more Vanished immediately fell upon him, tackling him. Farfin tried to come to his aid but an ax bit deep into his neck. The shipbuilder stumbled and fell over the railing. Kirth grabbed both The Vanished atop him by their necks as they clawed at his face and stood. The large man squeezed. Delanis saw his brother's muscles bulge and heard the cartilage of The Vanished's necks crumple.

And still, more came, jumping and crawling to the Red Raven. Delanis's men cried out as The Vanished swarmed them, unable to resist the onslaught.

One by one, his men fell. Delanis spun into the fray, Kirth and Kerstin right behind him. They slashed and bashed, cutting limbs and heads free. Several Vanished rushed Kirth again, obviously sensing him to be the most lethal threat. Delanis was cut off from him as he contended with his own attackers, struggling mightily to protect Kerstin, though she fared well enough on her own. The pile upon Kirth grew until Delanis lost sight of him.

"Kirth!"

Delanis tried in vain to cut his way to his brother. *"Kirth!"* The pile erupted as Kirth rose, bellowing and swearing, arrayed in flowing crimson.

"By Vyath and all the gods, I will send you back to the Plains of Kulbrar!" Blood streamed from a score of gashes and rips on his body, and one of his eye sockets was empty. Still, Kirth fought on, clearing the ground before him with his bare hands. And then, he went rigidly still mid-stride.

"No!" Delanis cried.

A metal blade spurted out Kirth's chest. He slumped to his knees. Behind Kirth stood a small figure with a slender hand upon the hilt of the sword.

Orra.

Kirth smiled a bloody grin. "I'm sorry, Brother." He fell forward, face first into the deck, and went still.

The sight of Orra slowed time for Delanis. Her skin, even in the light of first moon, was pale, drawn too tight. Her cheek bones angled more sharply than natural. But it *was* her.

"What have you done?"

"Delanis!" Kerstin cried.

He ducked a lethal blow and nearly clove The Vanished's face in two as he swung his ax up and through its chin in reprisal. It died silently, as the rest of its sick kin had.

Orra stood still upon his ship, gazing down at him, a placid smile on her lips, while the other Vanished swarmed the ship.

A shriek cut the sky above, a roar that Delanis recognized. The Vanished recoiled, ducking their heads with yellow eyes turned toward the sky. Another shriek and The Vanished scrambled back to their ship, climbing over each other in a frenzied stampede. Orra, however, stood still.

"I'm sorry, Dada. Mother made me. I didn't want to."

The roar came again, more this time. Dozens shook the air as echoes reverberated off the glacial walls. Mist started to swallow The Vanished's ship, as if hiding it from what would come. From above, something streaked through the fog, straight down to the ship of The Vanished, hitting with the sound of a crashing boulder. More followed. The reports of snapping wood and screams penetrated the mist. The Vanished did not die silently now.

Delanis knelt at Kirth's side. His brother was indeed dead, unmoving. Delanis shut his eyes against the pain of loss.

"Why are you here!" Delanis screamed at Orra. "What do you want?"

"She cannot hold me completely, Dada. She broke the rules to get to you."

Eyrna's mercy, what is this? Orra's voice was heartbreakingly thin and weak, sluggish.

Splashes, bodies hitting the water sounded from the mist. Above, the flying demons attacked The Vanished upon their frozen ledges as well. To the port side, a large body, that of an alysaar from Delanis's Sighting, toppled into the water. Orra flinched.

"The alysaar prey upon us. They cannot abide the Influence in our blood. It is anathema to them."

"What rules?" Delanis demanded, ignoring her strange comments about the alysaars and Influence within blood, and the fact that Orra did not know the word "anathema." "Of what do you speak?"

"One per family. The Living Light limits Her claim to one per family."

One? Selirra. The Vanishing had already taken Selirra.

"Mother broke the rules when you didn't follow Mama. Mother had to take me, as well. But She can't hold me, not completely."

One *claim* per family. "But I could voluntarily seek her."

Orra smiled wider, as if truly happy. "Yes."

"Delanis," Kerstin whispered. "It's not her."

"If I come . . . this Mother will then have all three of us!"

Orra smiled so condescendingly that Delanis knew it was not hers. "She will release Mama and me if you seek her."

It is true, Throne Delanis of Ishalar, Noxmyra sang in his mind.

An alysaar slammed into the Red Raven's deck with a thud, the bony mass at the end of the tail shattering the wooden planks as no more than the papery bark of a white pine. The creature rose up on its hind legs, towering over Orra and jutting the bladed spikes that protruded from its chin at her in warning. The ship titled starboard violently. Kerstin fell into Delanis, and they both stumbled into the railing. The alysaar stepped toward Orra with a thunderous screech. Orra stumbled, her face even more ashen.

"Dada . . ."

"No!" Delanis said. "Stop!"

The alysaar craned its head to look at Delanis. He shook his head. "Please, not her."

The beast lowered its hind legs, and again the ship rocked. Delanis did not hesitate. He grabbed Kerstin by the wrist and pulled her with him as he climbed upon the alysaar's back. Orra's shift tore slightly as he hauled her up as well. His daughter struggled, going into a fit, clawing and fighting, foaming at the mouth; but Delanis clamped her limbs tightly. The girl *seethed* in his arms.

Delanis opened his Immortal Eye and connected to the alysaar. *Rise.*

The alysaar's wings unfurled, and it leaped from the deck, gaining lift. As they rose above the fray, Delanis took in the aerial view. Scores of alysaars emerged from the thickening fog, trailing wisps of the gray vapor, then dove again into the mist like arrows shot from Vyath's bow.

Delanis hugged the alysaar under him with his legs as it banked hard to the left. Kertsin swore and reached under Delanis's arms to help secure Orra. His daughter squirmed more ferociously as they climbed higher from The Vanished's den. Three arrows raced past them and the alysaar banked hard again. Delanis's stomach lurched. The Vanished on the higher ledges of the glacier hurled spears and threw axes. Delanis ducked, covering Orra. She snapped at his face, like a feral wolf. Delanis barely moved in time.

"I'm sorry, Dada," she whispered through quivering lips. Whatever possessed her, she was fighting it.

Delanis pressed his hand to Orra's forehead, his thumb finding the link to her sentient core at the bridge of her nose. Before him appeared a Sighting of a foreign land, one of obsidian terrain masked in a blue murkiness not unlike the fog upon the waters. In the midst of the murkiness stood a woman of such exquisite grace that Delanis's breath caught. He flinched as the Sighting focused on her completely, the black landscape fading to obscureness.

Seek me, Delanis, Throne of Ishalar, for I am near. I am a kind God.

Inexplicably, he lifted his gaze to that of first moon though still enraptured by the Sighting. "By virtue of the authority granted me as a Throne of Ishalar by the Immortal Ones, I banish you from my daughter and this land!"

The woman laughed. *Your blood is my blood, Delanis. You are descended from il'Helosha, from my clan. Your gift of the Living Light fades as my Influence grows in you. Do not fret, Delanis, Throne of Ishalar, for I am kind. And I am coming.*

"I banish you!"

You cannot ever rid yourself of me. I am in you, your blood . . .

Delanis felt the truth of her words, and it enraged him. He felt something else swell within him, a surge of knowledge as he concentrated more on that side of him that harbored his gift, that side that breathed in concert with the Living Light, with that . . . "Influence" was the word that came to his mind . . . that Influence that the Immortal Ones had lived by before the Fracturing. The words, which he knew instantly to be Axioms of Light, came.

"Encriyo, esha vash dustánt, il'Helosha."

His Sighting shattered, the woman splintering into a million shards of glass as the world rematerialized to his eyes. Orra instantly sucked in a new breath, greedily taking air in several large gulps before going limp in her father's arms.

Away, Delanis said through his Immortal Eye. The alysaar climbed higher in the air, above the glaciers that seemed to scratch the sky, and turned west. Delanis felt his Eye close, and knew it was for the last time.

SEVEN

DELANIS DRIFTED BETWEEN WAKEFULNESS
and sleep with Kerstin leaning forward on his back.
He felt her slow, steady breathing and knew she
slept. They flew for nearly two days, avoiding the rift,
resting only for an hour half a dozen times on the
pillars that dotted the northern rim of the sea, east of
the Skithya Isles. By the time they reached Ishalar,
Delanis was weak with hunger. Orra had not stirred
the past half day at all, but seemed stronger, her
skin's natural hue returning, and her facial features
softening.

The alysaar landed on the beach. By Eyrna's mercy, there were no tracks.

"You must not live, Throne Delanis, for the world's sake." Girshkil's words rang in his mind. "You will become a conduit for the Dark . . ."

Will you wait? Delanis tried to ask the alysaar through his Immortal Eye, but it wouldn't open. The creature just stared at him with his furious black irises.

"My gift has left me. I no longer have Sight." Something remained though, the awakening of another part inside him. Something that beckoned him east. *The Luring.*

"But you—"

"It is a mercy," Delanis said. "I understand why the gods have taken it from us." *I will not be a conduit for the Dark to seep into this Living Light Girshkil spoke of.* He put his hand on the alysaar's scaly neck. "Wait. Please." After a moment, the alysaar sat on its hind legs, then collapsed down on the beach, breathing heavily.

"It's exhausted," Kerstin said.

"It will wait."

Delanis led them into town. Orra had roused herself somewhat and walked haphazardly. She accepted her father's hand as they walked, something that heartened Delanis immeasurably.

"Delanis, where is everyone?" Kerstin asked. "Why isn't anyone greeting us?"

Tumbleweeds rolled by as they strolled through the silent streets of Heina. No chatter of merchants or patter of feet found his ears.

"Come, we must see Throne Gaerrin," Delanis said.

As they turned the corner past Baelor's home, Delanis froze. The shadow on the outside of Baelor's house was gone. Gingerly, Delanis traced the area of the wall where the shadow had manifested then rubbed his fingers together. No soot. No ash. Was this new plaster? He inspected the rest of the wall. No, new plaster had not been applied. Certainly not recently.

"Mishya?" Delanis called. He knocked on the door. "Goshan?" He knocked again and the door creaked open. The house was empty. Delanis felt it in the air, the wrongness.

"Delanis . . ."

He knew what Kerstin was going to say. He ran to his house and burst through the threshold. Selirra's shadow was gone. *Vyath's blood, what is this?* For the grief it had brought him, the shadow's absence conjured a perplexing sorrow in him.

"Delanis!"

Kerstin's shout had come from several houses down. He sprinted outside, called to the empty streets. "Where are you?"

She stepped out of Proklam's house with Orra and waved to him. Orra had a fish in her hand.

"Here," Kerstin said.

Delanis ran quickly to her. "It's gone, isn't it? Shayleel's shadow?"

"Yes."

"Have you seen anyone at all?"

Kerstin shook her head.

They went from house to house but found exactly what Delanis had expected by now. Even the Hall of Thrones lay empty, neither Throne Gaerrin nor the other Thrones could be found.

No trace.

No tracks.

No shadows.

"Dada, we don't have much time."

Your blood is tainted . . .

"I know, Orra."

"They are coming."

"I know. I feel them."

"What? Who?" asked Kerstin.

"Those of il'Helosha. The Vanished. I feel their approach like a roiling in my blood. They have already come through the rift. I . . . I must leave."

Kerstin looked up sharply. "What do you mean?"

"Orra and I both. They will never stop seeking us. They think to invade the Living Light through my gift."

"But . . . you said it has left you."

"Mother is spiteful," Orra said.

"It will not matter," Delanis said. "Once they learn this, they will only try to kill Orra and me." He lifted a hand in front of his face. It tingled, on the edge of burning. "I feel them closer now." Delanis spun. "The beach!"

He dashed through the streets back toward the beach, his heart literally thudding against his chest. Only urgency drove him now as his body ached for nourishment. There, on the wet sand, he saw The Vanished climbing doggedly out the waters, single-mindedly attacking the alysaar, encircling it.

It whipped its tail, smashing the mace-like bolus at the end against dozens of Vanished. It whirled, slinging its maw into more Vanished, stabbing the blade-like chin spikes through flesh and bone. More Vanished poured from the sea, as if every new wave birthed another score.

"How are there so many?" Kerstin asked, breathless.

"The ocean. It provides cover for them against the alysaars. The Vanished do not need breath. Hurry!"

Kerstin took Orra's hand as they all ran onto the beach. The Vanished swarmed around the spinning alysaar.

"Here!" Delanis called. The alysaar spotted them, leaped over the growing crowd of Vanished and darted up the beach to them.

The Vanished lurched after it.

"Quickly!" Kerstin said, hoisting Orra onto the alysaar's back. Delanis jumped on next and pulled Kertsin up right behind him. They *snarled,* The Vanished, like a pack of mad jackals.

"Fly!" Delanis commanded.

The alysaar took flight, lumbering greatly to gain altitude.

Come on!

"Will this help?" Orra asked, holding out her fish. Delanis chuckled despite himself and took it. He threw it high in the air, and the alysaar lunged upward and caught it.

"Yes, Orra, I think it did help."

The Vanished grew small below them as they climbed, shrinking in size until the whirlpool clouds blocked them from view completely.

"Where are we going, Delanis?" Kerstin asked, leaning against his back and wrapping her arms around him with a grip that bespoke desperation and longing.

Delanis held his silence for several moments, unsure what to answer. He would have to run far, always hiding, perhaps until death took him. But he had a woman he loved, a daughter to raise, and perhaps some greater destiny to fulfill. That thought rooted itself deeply within him. He took Kerstin's hand as the alysaar flew higher and pressed it against his chest, interlocking his fingers with hers. "Wherever the quiescent currents lead us, even if to the edge of the world."

Girshkil had mentioned a name, hadn't he? Someone who had sent him to "watch" the people of Ishalar? *Chaimere il'Kiarra, the last . . . of your Immortal Ones, Girshkil had said.* This Chaimere obviously knew something about what had befallen

Delanis's people and sent an assassin among them . . . instead of help. Delanis gripped the ax haft at his waist as they sailed through another whirlpool cloud, leaving his skin and clothes damp. Yes, he would seek out this Chaimere of Clan Kiarra, last of the Ancients.

THE END

ABOUT THE AUTHOR

Jacob Cooper is an award-winning, #1 bestselling epic fantasy author. In addition to writing *The Dying Lands Chronicle*, his works have been included in several anthologies alongside other high-profile authors. His first effort, *Moon Monsters*, was written when he faked sickness one day in first grade to stay home and write. This story received the acclaim of his parents and sits in a black 3-ringed binder somewhere in their basement. Aside from writing, Jacob is an accomplished percussionist, pianist, and composer. He enjoys power sports on land and water, as well as spending time with his family.

www.circleofreign.com

Facebook.com/jacobcooperCOR
@AuthorJacobCoop